I'm learning about...

opposites

illustrated by REBECCA ARCHER

Ladybird

Armadillo's awake in the morning.

Ape's fast asleep at night.

awake asleep

Buffalo's big and heavy.

Ladybird's little and light.

heavy   light

Hyena is laughing. She's happy!

Kangaroo's crying. She's sad.

happy   sad

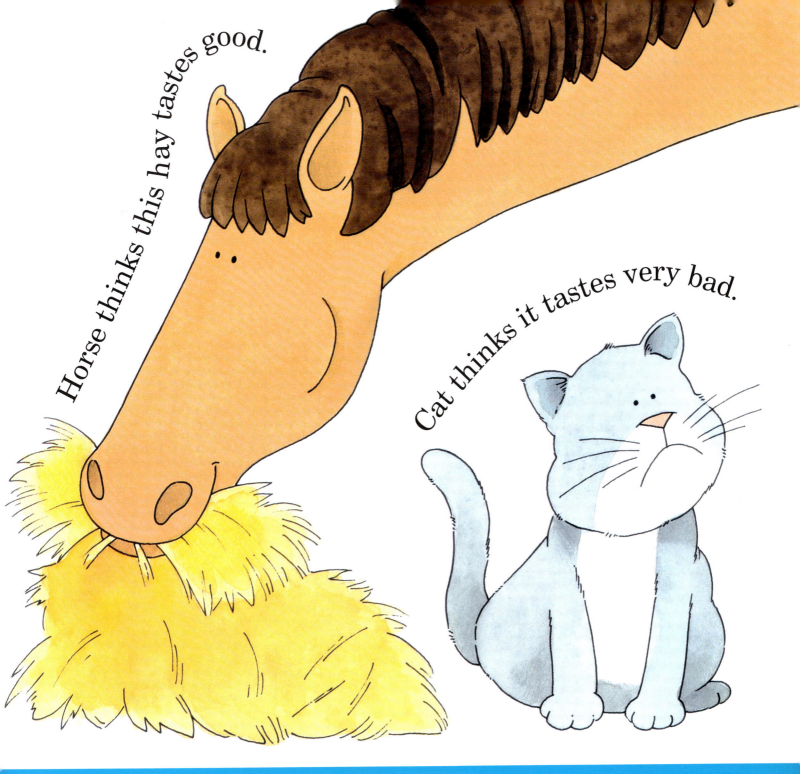

Horse thinks this hay tastes good.

Cat thinks it tastes very bad.

good   bad

Dog's been getting all dirty.

Panda, however, is clean!

dirty clean

Frog is as fat as a sausage.

Lizard's as thin as a bean.

fat   thin

Seal's skin is smooth, sleek and shiny.

Rhino's is wrinkled and rough.

smooth   rough

Elephant eats lots of ice cream.

For mouse, just a little's enough.

lots   a little

Camel is hot in the desert.

Polar Bear's cold in the snow.

hot   cold

Fox runs fast through the forest.

Snail, though, is sluggish and slow.

fast   slow

Beaver is busy with building.

Lion is lazy in bed.

busy 🐝 🐱 lazy

Rat scurries under the fence.

Goat jumps over instead.

under  over

Dolphin dives down and gets wet.

Badger jumps up and stays dry.

wet

dry

Cow looks down low for her dinner, while Giraffe finds hers way up high!

low high

Penguin walks proudly in front.

Skunk straggles far, far behind.

in front   behind

Otter is on the red wagon.

Hen's fallen off – never mind!

on  off

Leopard looks out on the left,

and Rabbit is there on the right.

left ⬅ ➡ right

One sheep is fluffy and black.

The other is fluffy and white!

black white

The policeman tells Squirrel to stop!

But Goose is ready to go!

stop   go

Ostrich's legs are quite long.

Duck's legs are quite short, as you know.

long   short

Bear has a very large pancake.

Owl has a very small pie.

large small

hello   goodbye

Big or small?

Which animals are big?
Which animals are small?

Hot or cold?

What will you wear when it's hot?
What will you wear when it's cold?

Wet or dry?

Can you point to the animals who are getting wet?

Which animals are staying dry?

Odd one out

Find the dog who is different from the rest.

Which bird is doing something different from the others?

In front or behind?

How many animals are in front of the fence?

How many are peeping out from behind?